Give

NURSE NIBBLES

her medical bag so she can make
the Get Well Friends better.

Cassie the Cat

Pedro the Penguin

Zoe the Zebra

Sonia the
Snow Rabbit

Paul the Python

Chesney the Cheetah

Emo the Elephant

Beyonce the Bear

Nurse Nibbles

George the
Giant Snail

Giselle the Giraffe

Momo the Monkey

BUT THEY ALL TOOK THEIR MEDICINE,
AND THEY ALL GOT BETTER IN...

She sneezed and set fire to her jumper.

Delia the dragon is poorly.

She broke her tooth biting a rhino's bottom.

Connie the crocodile is poorly.

She crashed into a wall,
chasing mice.

Cassie the cat is poorly.

A gorilla tied him in a knot.

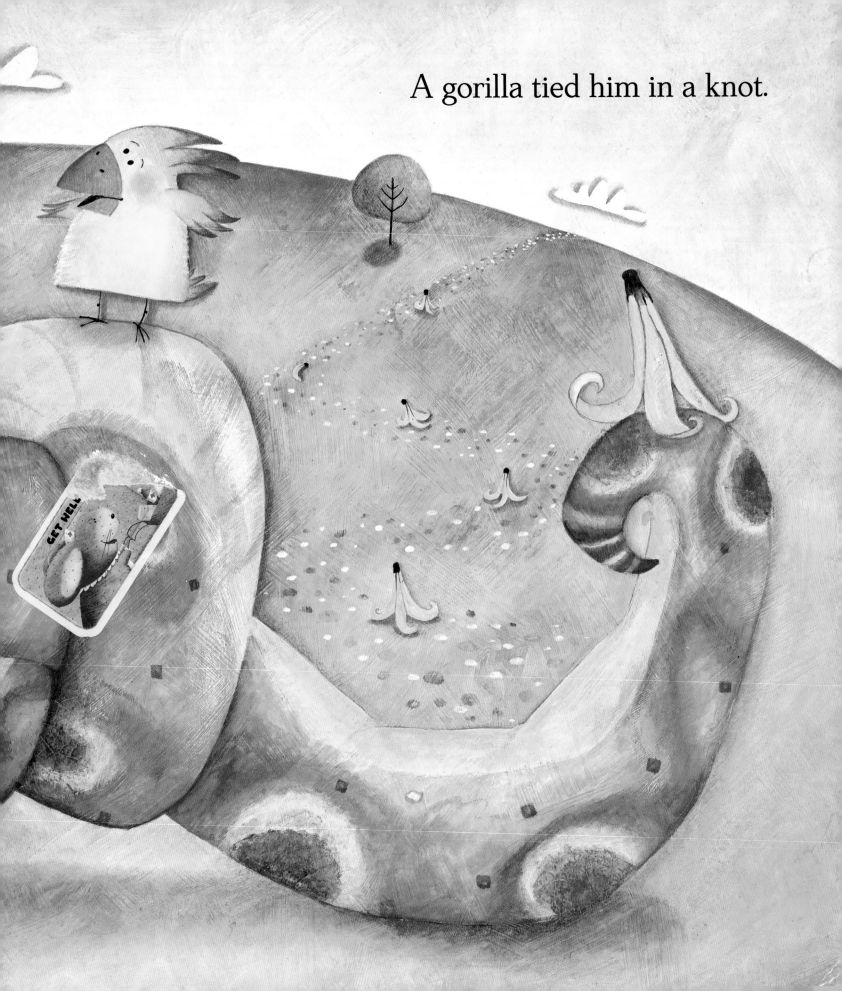

Paul the python is poorly.

His spots came out in stripes.

Dipak the Dalmatian is poorly.

He tunnelled straight into a well.

Morgan the mole is poorly.

An elephant trod on her shell.

Tiffany the tortoise is poorly.

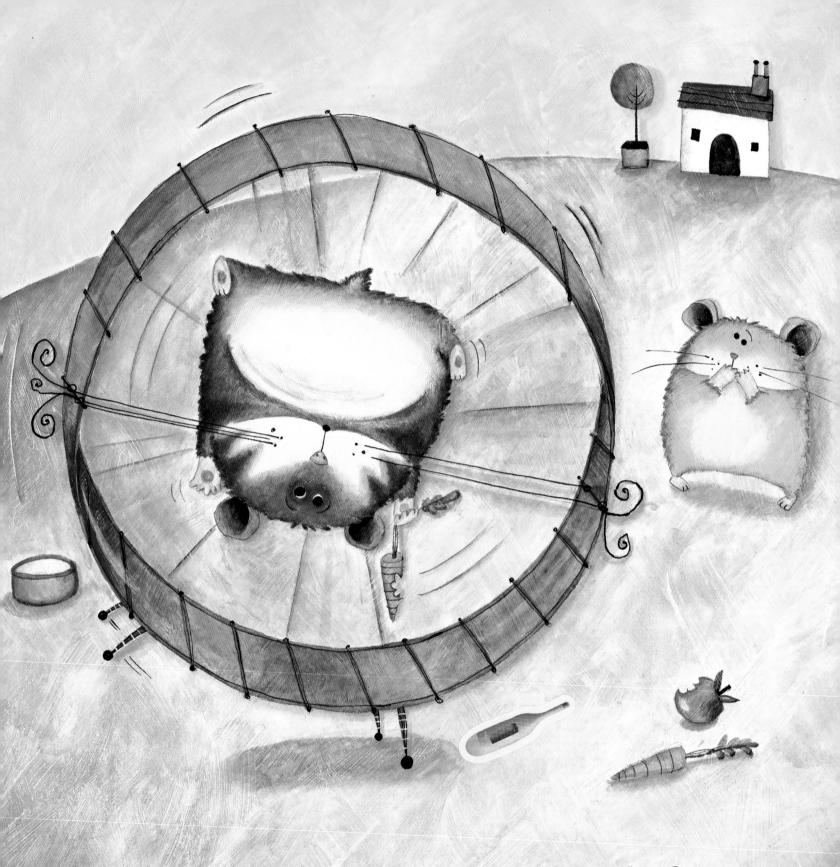

He got his whiskers caught up in his wheel.

Hamish the hamster is poorly.

She sprained 98 ankles playing hockey.

First published in hardback in 2011 by Hodder Children's Books
This edition published in 2012
Copyright © Get Well Friends Ltd.

WWW.GETWELLFRIENDS.COM

Hodder Children's Books, 338 Euston Road, London, NW1 3BH
Hodder Children's Books Australia, Level 17/207 Kent Street, Sydney, NSW 2000

The right of Kes Gray to be identified as the author and Mary McQuillan as the illustrator
of this Work has been asserted by them in accordance with the Copyright, Designs and Patents Act 1988.

A catalogue record of this book is available from the British Library.

ISBN: 9781 444 90382 9

Hodder Children's Books is a division of Hachette Children's Books
An Hachette UK Company
www.hachette.co.uk

Cassie the Cat

Pedro the Penguin

Zoe the Zebra

Chesney the Cheetah

Sonia the
Snow Rabbit

Paul the Python

Emo the Elephant

Beyonce the Bear

Nurse Nibbles

Momo the Monkey

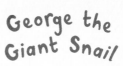

George the
Giant Snail

Giselle the Giraffe